MR. SILLY™
on the FARM

Library of Congress Cataloging in Publication Data

Hargreaves, Roger.
  Mr. Silly on the farm.

  (The Mr. men word books)
  Summary: Mr. Silly and his friends come to help Farmer Plough on the farm, but they don't accomplish what they've set out to do. Includes word lists.
  [1. Humorous stories] I. Title.
PZ7.H2226Mrr 1981   [E]   81-13882
ISBN 0-86592-586-0   AACR2

Rourke Enterprises, Inc.
Windermere, Florida 32786

walked
path
frightened
geese
instead
scared

Mr. Silly and his friends came to the
farm. They wanted to help Farmer Plow.

Mr. Silly walked up the path to the
farmhouse. Suddenly, something came
rushing toward him.

It was Mr. Jelly. He was very frightened.

Farmer Plow had given him some bread.
He was told to feed the geese.
Mr. Jelly thought they were going to eat
him instead.

"Do not be scared," said Mr. Silly.
"Geese do not eat people. They like ice
cream."

field
counting
sheep
moved
idea
loose

Mr. Silly saw Mr. Dizzy in a field. He was counting the sheep.

"One, two, six, four . . ." counted Mr. Dizzy.

One of the sheep moved. Mr. Dizzy lost count. He had to start again.

Mr. Silly had an idea.

"Why don't you open the gate? Count the sheep as they come out" he said.

Soon Mr. Dizzy had counted six sheep. They were all running loose in the road. Farmer Plow was not very pleased.

through
strange
knows
annoyed
safely
hedge

In the next field Mr. Silly found a big
bull. It had a ring through its nose.

"What a strange place to wear a ring,"
thought Mr. Silly. "Everyone knows that
you wear rings on your toes."

Mr. Silly walked up to the bull and said, "Baa baa!"

The bull was a bit annoyed. He ran after Mr. Silly. Mr. Silly ran away as fast as he could. He did not stop until he was safely on the other side of the hedge.

push
tractor
drive
pointed
wheels
almost

Mr. Silly met Farmer Plow's men.
They were trying to push a tractor.
   "Why don't you drive it instead?"
said Mr. Silly.
   The men pointed to the front wheels
of the tractor. They were stuck in the mud.

Just then Mr. Strong came along the
road. With one hand he lifted the tractor
out of the mud. Then, he carried it back to
the farm.

He was strong! The men were pleased.
They almost forgot to thank Mr. Strong.

collect
basket
broken
sixth
slipped
twice

Mr. Silly went to the hen house. He found Mr. Clumsy helping the farmer's wife collect the eggs.

Mr. Clumsy had only three eggs in his basket. There were five broken eggs on the ground.

"Whoops!" said Mr. Clumsy for the sixth
time. Another egg slipped out of his
hand.

The farmer's wife was angry. So were
the hens! They would have to lay almost
twice as many eggs the next day.

pigpen
dirty
piglet
hose
turned
sprayed

Mr. Silly went to the pigpen. It was
very dirty. He started to clean it.
Soon, Mr. Silly was as dirty as the pigs.
 "Quack quack!" said Mr. Silly to a piglet.
 "Eek!" said the piglet, and ran away.
Mr. Silly picked up a hose.

Just then, Mr. Mischief came along.
He turned on the faucet. Wooosh!
Water sprayed all over Mr. Silly.
Mr. Silly was very wet. So were the pigs!
The pigpen was covered with water.

bring
milking
wool
cream
finger
licked

Mr. Silly helped Farmer Plow bring in the
cows. It was time for milking.

"Does wool come from cows?" asked
Mr. Silly.

"Don't be silly," said the farmer. "Milk
comes from cows. Wool comes from
sheep."

Inside, Mr. Greedy was helping the farmer's wife. She was making cream. Mr. Greedy put his finger in the cream and licked it. The farmer's wife was angry. She sent Mr. Greedy away. She asked Mr. Silly to help her instead.

vegetable
digging
easy
holding
asleep
cabbages

Mr. Silly was at the back of the farmhouse. He had found a vegetable garden.

Mr. Topsy Turvy was digging in the soil. This was not an easy thing to do. He was holding his spade upside down.

16

Mr. Lazy was asleep. He was lying at the
end of a row of cabbages.

"Good morning Mr. Topsy Turvy!"
shouted Mr. Silly.

"Silly morning Mr. Good," said Mr. Topsy
Turvy. He went on digging.

orchard
picking
branch
climbed
stepped
squashed

Mr. Silly went into the orchard. Mr. Tall was picking apples. Mr. Tall was very tall. He could stand on the ground and reach the highest apples.

Mr. Silly picked a shiny red apple from a branch. He was about to bite it. Something was wrong. It walked out of his hand.

18

It was Mr. Small! He had climbed the tree. He did not want to be stepped on. Mr. Small asked Mr. Silly to put him on the fence.

"Now I will not get squashed or eaten," said Mr. Small.

farmyard
fruit
choose
soup
pour
roast

Farmer Plow had a shop in the farmyard. He used it to sell food from the farm.

He sold vegetables, fruit, cream, and eggs.

Mr. Silly started to choose some things. He found some apples to make soup. He bought some cream to pour over his roast beef.

Then, he picked up a cabbage.

"This is just what I need. I will use it to clean my windows," said Mr. Silly.

mess
flooded
spoiled
dirty
worry
tomorrow

It was time for Mr. Silly and his
friends to go. Farmer Plow looked
around at the mess.

There were still some sheep running
loose in the road. There were broken eggs

in the hen house. The pigpen was flooded.
And, Mr. Greedy had spoiled the cream.
He should not have put his dirty fingers in it.

"Do not worry," said Mr. Silly. "We will
come and help you again tomorrow!"

Questions to talk about

1. Why was Mr. Jelly frightened?
2. Why do you think the bull wears a ring through his nose?
3. How many eggs did Mr. Clumsy break?
4. Who turned on the hose?
5. Why was the farmer's wife angry at Mr. Greedy?
6. What would you buy to make soup?
7. Is Farmer Plow happy they are coming back?